ALMOST GOOD-BYE

by Helen Cresswell
and Judy Brown

DUTTON CHILDREN'S BOOKS

NEW YORK

Speedsters is a trademark of Dutton Children's Books.

Text copyright © 1990 by Helen Cresswell
Illustrations copyright © 1990 by Judy Brown

Library of Congress Cataloging-in-Publication Data
Cresswell, Helen.
  Almost good-bye / by Helen Cresswell and Judy Brown.—1st
American ed.
    p. cm.
  Summary: While collecting things to sell at a school White
Elephant sale, two friends are given a lamp with unexpected
magic qualities.
  ISBN 0-525-44858-6
  [1. Magic—Fiction.] I. Brown, Judy, ill. II. Title.
PZ7.C8645Al 1992   91-33464
[Fic]—dc20   CIP
                                                   AC

First published in the United States 1992 by Dutton Children's Books,
a division of Penguin Books USA Inc.
375 Hudson Street, New York, New York 10014

Originally published as *Almost Goodbye Guzzler* in Great Britain 1990 by
A & C Black (Publishers) Ltd., London

First American Edition   Printed in U.S.A.
10 9 8 7 6 5 4 3 2 1

Susie Potts and Gumball Gumford were best friends.

So were their mothers.

Mrs. Potts and Mrs. Gumford talked about this so much, it was amazing that Susie and Gumball weren't worst enemies.

Susie and Gumball were in the fourth grade at Witherspoon Elementary School.

Their teacher was Miss Toasty. She was very very very very boring.

So Susie and Gumball sat at the back of
the room and did their own thing.

They played tic-tac-toe

or hangman

or mad libs.

Miss Toasty met...
Batman
In the... bathroom
She said..."Do you like my whiskers?"
He said..."with salt & pepper"
What she did: She sneezed six billion 467 times.
What he did: He chewed a ratburger.
What happened: A shark ate them and then burped.

They had fun all day, giggling and chewing on gumballs, while Miss Toasty droned on and on and on.

One day Miss Toasty rapped on her desk with a ruler. The class looked up—even Susie and Gumball.

"I have some very exciting news!" she said.

"Next Saturday we are holding a school fair!" Miss Toasty said. "And our class will be in charge of the White Elephant stand!"

"A white elephant is something that you don't want anymore," Miss Toasty went on. "But it may be exactly what someone else wants."

"And then you can go around to your neighbors," Miss Toasty said.

"You must be very polite, and you must work in pairs."

"Gumball and me!" yelled Susie.

"I think," said Miss Toasty, "that some people in the back are being silly."

The fourth graders of Witherspoon Elementary School went knocking on doors and ringing doorbells.

Abdul Singh and Julie Boot were in charge of the wagon.

Up and down the streets they pushed it. Into the wagon went . . .

rusty cages

torn cushions...

jigsaw puzzles with half the pieces missing...

babies' rattles with no rattles in them...

broken toasters...

YOU NAME IT!!

13

Miss Toasty was delighted. You could tell by the way she clapped her hands.

Wonderful! Keep it up!

Susie Potts and Gumball Gumford went off on their own. They wanted to collect more white elephants than the rest of the class put together.

They decided to try mostly old people. "I'll bet the older you are, the more white elephants you've got," said Susie.

(Susie and Gumball's manners were
very good when they wanted them to be.)

Mrs. Lane was very old, and she lived alone.

Inside her house it was very dark. The walls were covered with pictures. The rooms were crowded with pots and knickknacks.

It looked as if Mrs. Lane's whole house was a white elephant.

Mrs. Lane got some milk and cookies. That was fine with Susie and Gumball.

The cookies were gone fast.

Susie fed a cookie to Ermintrude because she liked to watch the parrot's beak move. It seemed to be on hinges.

"I remember when Alfred bought this from an antique shop when we were first married," Mrs. Lane told them. "I'm afraid it's rather dusty. Everything's dusty. My old hands are too shaky to dust these days."

"How very kind," said Mrs. Lane. "Thank you."

Susie and Gumball really were nice kids.

They thanked Mrs. Lane and promised to come next week to do the dusting. Then they left with the lamp.

THE LAMP

Susie and Gumball went and sat in the park while they decided where to knock next. They stared at the one thing they had collected so far.

It was easy to see why the lamp was a white elephant. What would anyone use it for?

And it certainly was dusty. Gumball gave it a rub.

Gumball's mind was a total blank. So was Susie's.

They were stunned.

Shocked.

Awestruck.

They gazed up at the genie in his swirl of blue-and-green smoke.

"I am the genie of the lamp. You have two wishes left!" he said.

Two wishes? Was this a dream?

Wishes! You just don't go around expecting to have wishes granted. No one does. Maybe we should all carry a card with three wishes written on it. Then we'd be ready for emergencies. Susie and Gumball were not ready.

The genie disappeared in a puff of
smoke and a loud *whoosh*.

Gumball and Susie blinked.

Had they imagined the whole thing?

Gumball was gone. Almost.

His clothes were empty.

Neither of them could believe it.

At first, Gumball was thrilled to be invisible.

He wanted to...

stick his tongue out
at Miss Toasty...

go through every door that said
NO STUDENTS...

and best of all . . .

Gumball ran off. He had big plans.
Susie went after him.

Just then, a hobo came shuffling through the park.

He stared, he shook his head, then he stared again.

He had seen plenty of strange things in his time, but never anything like this.

Gumball Gumford ran out of the park and into the street.

After him went Susie Potts.

She wished she had her camera with her. No one was ever going to believe this.

There's one good thing, Susie thought. At least he can use the last wish to become visible again!

BUT CAN HE ???...

The poor hobo thought he'd better sit down after such a shock.

MORAL

Don't litter and don't leave magic lamps around.

( )

[Especially when they give three wishes, and you've already used up two.]

A pair of grubby sneakers, some blue jeans, and a T-shirt were moving up Witherspoon Road. Even though Gumball's legs were invisible, they still worked.

Chasing after Gumball was Susie Potts, who by now had a stitch in her side. She had such a bad stitch, she thought she might end up in the hospital.

The police will never believe this!

So did some other people who spotted the headless, armless, and legless Gumball.

Gumball raced on, straight for the girls' bathroom.

His mind was working fast.

He wondered if he really was like a ghost and could go through things. He decided to test it on a lamppost.

Gumball rubbed the invisible bump on
his invisible nose.

He wondered if he needed an invisible
Band-Aid.

At last Susie caught up.

"This is terrific," Gumball told her.
"Where's Miss Toasty?"

I keep trying to tell you! I can still see your CLOTHES!!

WHO CARES?

He certainly didn't.

No one will know it's me.

Then you'll have to use your last wish to become visible again.

Susie was getting fed up.

That was when the awful

THE AWFUL

The lamp! Where is it?

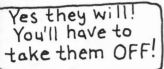

Yes they will! You'll have to take them OFF!

Gumball stared with his invisible eyes.

WHAT?! And go around naked? No way!

truth dawned on them.

TRUTH

I thought you had it!

SHOCK HORROR

The hobo had no idea what the lamp
was for. He just hoped it would be worth
a dollar or two. He picked it up.

Susie thought fast. She saw the kids playing soccer.

"Quick—get behind that tree!" she told Gumball. She went over to the kids. "Hey, did you take a lamp off this bench?" she asked them.

Gumball then made a

MAJOR ERROR.

He came out from behind the tree. Poor Gumball didn't realize what a scary sight he was.

"A hobo? Where did he go?" he demanded.

When the kids saw him, they went into a

HELP!

It's a phantom T-shirt!

RUN FOR IT!!

CHAMP

Susie and Gumball were now in a serious mess. It looked as though a hobo had walked off with the lamp—and the genie! And there was only one wish left!!!

Meanwhile, the panic-stricken kids had gone to dial 911.

Susie and Gumball raced off. They had to find that hobo before he made a wish.

By now Gumball was beginning to wish he had taken off his clothes.

At least he'd be totally invisible if he were naked.

He was attracting too much attention.

The hobo went plodding along. He had no idea that he had a genie to command. He could have wished for a million dollars, if only he had known. He could have wished for a zillion.

He could have wished to grow wings or to breathe fire.

But soon he was tired again, so he started to look for a bus shelter.

Oh, my feet are killing me! Wish I had a—a...

...a...

...a...

By now the police were arriving on the scene. Their switchboard had been jammed with calls. They could not make head or tail of them, but they came to investigate anyway.

How are we goin to put handcuff on that!

Susie and Gumball heard the police. It looked as if they were through. They raced on—but it was too late. The police had spotted them.

Then, at the last instant,
Susie and Gumball saw
the hobo.

He was just going into the bus shelter. They sped up until they were breaking Olympic records.

The police jumped out of their cars and went after them. They were wondering how they would arrest a T-shirt and what to charge it with.

Before the hobo could finish his sentence, Susie and Gumball dashed toward him.

"There it is!" yelled Gumball, and he grabbed the lamp.

But the hobo was too late. He'd missed his chance. No million, no zillion. Nothing.

56

There was another WHOOSH with a puff of green-and-blue smoke. The genie was gone, and Gumball was back. After a moment's stunned silence, everyone was talking at once.

The police had a lot of trouble figuring out what had happened—or rather, *not* figuring it out because they never did. The police can't go around believing in magic lamps and wishes. So, in the end, they decided to forget the whole thing and let everybody off with a warning.

The school fair at Witherspoon Elementary was a great success.

Susie and Gumball handed the lamp over to Miss Toasty.

They were actually quite pleased to be rid of it. It never even occurred to them that the next person to have it would get three wishes too...

At the sale, Miss Toasty herself bought the lamp for a dollar.

Miss Toasty hurried off to put the lamp in her desk so that no one else would try to buy it. But she didn't really trust her class to be responsible while she was gone.

"At times like this," she said, "I wish I had two pairs of hands..."